S0-FAI-126

EVERYTHING BECAUSE OF TEETH

Luba Borochok

PUBLISH AMERICA

PublishAmerica
Baltimore

© 2003 by Luba Borochok.

All rights reserved. No part of this book may be reproduced, stored in a retrieval system or transmitted in any form or by any means without the prior written permission of the publishers, except by a reviewer who may quote brief passages in a review to be printed in a newspaper, magazine or journal.

First printing

ISBN: 1-4137-0838-2
PUBLISHED BY
PUBLISHAMERICA, LLLP.
www.publishamerica.com
Baltimore

Printed in the United States of America

*To my two wonderful children Robert and Anastasia
with hope that this story will help them to appreciate,
cherish, and preserve American freedom and our way of life.*

Acknowledgments

I would like to thank to the most extraordinary person in my life—my husband for support and encouragement, for his useful comments and suggestions, for reviewing this story as many times as I have, and for never doubting or giving up on me.

Special thanks goes to my dear professor, Dr. Wertime, who taught me everything I know about fiction, who helped me turn my thoughts into words, who discovered a quality in me I never thought I had, who believed in me when I did not believe that I could possibly write a fictional story, and who made himself available to me every time I needed.

I ALWAYS KNEW MY father loved me, but I seriously doubted whether I ever had any love for him until I was leaving my home and country for America. I could say I had a lot of feelings towards him; I just did not and could not know how to love him because in my eyes he was as hard as a rock. He never played with me when I was a child. I do not even remember him ever holding me in his hands or giving me a piggyback ride. Of course, he did not have time to play because he was a farmer. In the place where I came from, the former Soviet Union, farmers do not have time to fool around with their kids or play Hollywood; they have to take care of their farms and be prepared for very long and cold five-month winters. Otherwise, they and their animals would starve or, as they say in Russia, put their teeth on the shelves for the entire season. It always took the whole spring, summer, and fall to prepare for winter, but how could I, a six-year-old child, have understood that? Maybe I could have, but he never explained.

I was a gifted child. I understood many things even though I was never able to find out what my gift was; I only knew that it was prophesied to me on the day of my birth. The mystery of my beginning was almost like a fairy tale.

I was born in the smallest and last village of the USSR. It was the last village in all senses, ending the Soviet Union, but at the same time beginning and opening the road to Eastern Europe—right across the hill, where Poland began. Because no tourist was ever allowed to visit our village, our government did not need to show off our achievements. Therefore, we had no highways, no high buildings, and no public transportation. If we needed to travel to the city, we had to walk seven kilometers to the next village in order to catch a bus. Not many people knew about our village since it was not even on the map. Perhaps for that reason I never liked geography classes while in school because, instead of showing my own village on the map, I had to point at the one that was next to it. Other villagers laughed at us, saying that we were forgotten by people and God.

But God had not entirely abandoned us because he had awarded us with the most breathtaking landscapes I have ever seen in my life—valleys, plains, and hills covered with mountains of wild white and yellow daffodils and tulips in the spring; ruby and purple poppies, pansies, and violets in the summer; and golden and milky ox-eyed daisies, chrysanthemums, and zinnias in the fall. Nobody ever planted or took any special care of them; they just kept coming back to us every year. Even herbs, mints, dragon-flies, and dandelions that found themselves at home on our planting fields appeared attractive from the distance because of their special hues—in some places sapphire, in some rosy from mint's blossom, in others saffron from buttercups.

Because our village was no more than three kilometers long, it was virtually buried in greenery. Almost nothing there was lifeless or colorless, except for our main road, which looked gray; it was the only place without any vegetation. On both sides of that cheerless road there stood a chain of small red-roofed houses—about a hundred of them—each painted in either soft blue, cream, or light brown color. Even though we had tons of open space, our houses were built, practically, on top of each other, which could have been because of our harsh history.

Centuries ago barbarians—Mongolo-Tatars—used to attack our village from time to time, so my people had to stay close together in order to protect themselves. By the time we got our independence from all kinds of enemies, including Francas, Austrians, and Pollocks, we had gotten so used to living in each other's bedrooms that we did not want to change anything. And we continued building our houses in one another's yards side by side. Much later, in the twentieth century, spoiled by a few years of independence and freedom, people started to complain about not having enough backyard for their kids. But it was too late because one morning they woke up, and their country and land did not belong to them any more. Even though it was called the people's land, they still could not have it—only that portion for which the government did not find any use. So they had to stay in the same place where they had been for centuries.

But even with its small houses closely packed together, ours was still an appealing village. It was situated in a canyon of the green mountains. From the nearby hill it looked as though our village lay inside some sun-flowered bowl. On one side, the mountains were filled with pine and fir forests, on the other—with oak and birches. Surrounded by those birches and firs, I finally came into my village. I liked our weeping birches because they gave me and many others like me birch sap every early spring. At the end of March, when the snow was just about to disappear, we kids used to go to the woods with small glass jars and pocketknives to get birch sap. It was enough to put a tiny hole in the birch, and the sap would start seeping out into our jars. Only when our jars were half filled with sap did we leave the forest. At home we mixed it with water and sugar so we could immediately drink our birch juice, which had a bit crispy but at the same time soft taste of Pepsi's *Mountain Dew*. Even its pigment was fairly green. We were proud of ourselves because we made it with our own hands.

On the day I was born, one old dying lady, who was brought to our hospital from another village and whom my mother had never even met before, told her that some day I would be an important and well-known person. In fact, I was famous already on the day of my birth because I was the first child in the village who was delivered in our new hospital and not at home like the others who had come into the world before me.

For generations, even centuries, children in our village had been delivered by their mothers somewhere in the hay, under stalks of corn or in the wheat, and those more sophisticated or a bit richer inside their homes; I started a new trend. After me every child in our village was born in the hospital. It was even mandatory. The women actually liked it because they had to stay in the hospital for the entire week. It was free. It was their vacation, and they could truly rest by staying, perhaps for the first time in their lives, in bed until lunchtime without having to prepare food themselves but having it delivered to them on a silvered tray, instead.

There was an article about me in our county's local newspaper. My mother cut it out and put it in a frame. I am pretty certain that she still possesses it. But there were only two sentences about me. The rest of the article told a story about our village and how successful it had become since we had prospered so much. The article did not mention, of course, that my mother had had to share the same room with four other men and women and the dying lady, but maybe it was meant to be that way. Maybe the dying woman was there to deliver a message; at least my mother believed so.

Before the old lady died, she took me from my mother's hands, looked at my fingers, and said, "This shall be a special child. She possesses long and bending fingers. She shall be famous some day." After those words, she handed me back to my mother and died on the same day. My mother never forgot this story. And by the time I was six, I knew this story better than my mother. She was truly convinced that the old lady was right because when I earned my first A in the fourth grade, my mother told me that she had never had any doubt whether the prophecy of the old lady was correct. She never even forced me to study; she just knew that I was born to be a person worthy of a "capital letter," as she used to say.

The whole village knew this story, and they too looked at me as if I was a famous person already. I was never spanked by my next-door neighbor when I trampled his hay, as the rest of my friends were. Our other neighbors never threatened to let their dog off of the leash at me when I got in their garden and stole a cucumber. And even the most crazy person in our village, a 6'4" 200-pound blacksmith nicknamed "Ridiculous Stephen," never chased me out of our local and only supermarket, but gave me a penny once because I agreed to give him one tootsie roll. I was not alone of course; I was with my father. I remember holding so tightly to his pants that one could see his muscles from it. After that I could walk freely on our main street, but not the other kids, not even my younger brother.

Every day at about noon a swarm of kids, my brother included, would race down our street as they fled from Ridiculous Stephen, shouting so loud that the mothers would leave their kitchens, the fathers their stables to gallop outside in order to find out whether someone was torturing their kids. The kids were packed together so closely that they kept banging into one another, each trying to outrun the one who managed to be a foot ahead. They ran and ran and did not know when to stop. Frequently they ended up by our door because our house was the closest to the road and right before a hill. My mother often begged Ridiculous Stephen not to scare the children, but he just laughed and then took out a knife from his pocket and promised to cut off all of their tongues to make a galantine for himself. After hearing his words, the kids hollered even louder, some held on to my mother's skirt, my brother clung to her hips, others quickly ran to their mommies, and did not come outside for two hours. He even got me worried sometimes, and I too tried to stay close to my mother's skirt despite the fact that I was way over eight. But most of the time he patted me on the head and pledged not to cut off my tongue.

At first the parents were sensitive to their children's fear, but after a while they ignored their screams. They knew that if there was more than one child's scream on the street, that meant that Ridiculous Stephen was driving home from work for lunch. Years later, when some of the kids had grown smarter and the new ones took the place of the old crowd, he got tired of chasing them. One day he got off his horse, trapped about five kids in his arms, and instead of cutting off their tongues, picked up all of them at once high up into the air, and dropped them into his carriage to give them a ride over the hill. The rest of the kids, those he could not grab, jumped in by themselves. After that day they would not leave him alone and again ran through our street, screaming in the same way as before to be driven over the hill. Yet, even five years later after his death from cancer, he was still and always remembered as Ridiculous Stephen. That name just stuck to him. At the time when he was no longer ridiculous at all, our priest announced at his funeral, "Let us remember Ridiculous Stephen as a good-hearted, honest, and hard-working man."

***

Everybody knew the story of my birth. And as I grew, I got used to my special treatment by our village. While other kids were punched in their foreheads and had their ears twisted, I was patted on my head. I wonder

11

now whether people were extra generous to me so I would remember them when the vision of the old lady became a reality.

My father was the only person who was neither affected nor particularly impressed by the old lady's prophecy, and I did not like that. It never occurred to me to ask him why. But it did not occur to him either to provide me with such an answer even though we used to converse a lot with each other during my first six years of life. I even learned some things from him. He taught me everything about apples. I knew why I could not have them during the summer. It was wrong to eat apples before they were ripe because my stomach would hurt, and I would have to receive a lot of needles in my bottom. I also knew why I could not have too many apples in the fall because our family had to save them for the cold winter, and my mother needed to make a lot of different kinds of fruit pastes, thin jams, thick marmalades, and do canning so we would not be hungry during those chilly days.

I even tried not to throw too many rocks at the apple trees to knock off those apples that were unreachable with my bare hands. I often drooled, observing the red delicious apples, trying for hours to figure out how to get at least one down just to be able to bite into it.

Maybe because my father taught me too much about apples, I became obsessed with them. And all I did the whole day was trying to figure out how to pull one from the tree. Sometimes I managed to reach a few with a horse-rake; it did not always work, and most of the time I ended up with a broken branch rather than a red delicious. Rocks worked better because they were not strong enough to break the branch. Most importantly, I did not have to postpone eating an apple—if I had the luck to get one—in order to hide the broken branch first so my father would not discover it. That often spoiled my appetite. I was nervous about the branch, and I even looked differently at the apple. I glanced at it while biting it, and I even started to notice that the apples I knocked down were much more attractive on the outside than on the inside. For in their cores, there were worms, some white, some yellow, and some grayish, but all of them, with no exception, at least those that I observed, had black heads and tails.

My mother saw them too. Yet, all of us benefited from the black heads and tails during the canning season because it was much easier for my mother to see them inside at the time when she had to give each apple special treatment before it could be turned into preserved food. She cut every apple into eight pieces, and not one but three buckets were always in her use. One was on her right, so overflowing with apples that about ten of them fell to the floor and rolled all over the kitchen. Into another on her left she threw the peelings, seeds, the rotten apples, and worms. The third one was a nine-liter casserole on the table to hold the cut pieces. Sitting bent at a forty-five degree angle in a chair and holding a knife in her right hand very close to her chest, she used to say over and over again, "I got you, you black-headed devil." A lot of those black-headed devils would have ended up in our marmalades and jams had it not been for their conspicuous heads. Even with her poor vision my mother could still see them. I was not the only one.

No black-headed devil, though, could turn me away from apples, and the ones that I used to acquire by throwing rocks at them were the best. I called them the rocked apples. They were much softer and juicier, especially where they had been bruised. Many times I barely noticed or maybe did not wish to notice the worms. Even if I did, I did not care much about them at the time when saliva was running down my chain. I just bit off the piece with the worm in it, if there was one, spat it to the ground, and ate the rest of the apple with a clear mind, not worrying that some other smaller worm would go down along with a piece of apple and grow to become a big intestinal cystoid. I was pretty aware about intestinal worms because I used to have them almost as often as rain in Seattle.

Those intestinal worms just lived in me, and habitually, I myself, sitting on the toilet in the outhouse, saw them hanging from my butt.

I can still see myself sitting on that toilet, and I can still clearly picture our shanty. It was about six feet tall and four feet wide. To step into the outhouse, I needed to raise my right foot about two feet above the ground because it did not have stairs. Two one-foot-wide plywood planks served as a floor, but for some reason they were one inch apart from each other. I could easily slide three of my fingers in between them. Through that opening, underneath I could see waste and different kinds of flies and bugs. What the two boards could not cover, about two feet, remained a hole, which for a while functioned as our toilet. We certainly could not sit there at first. Instead, we had to step on the end of the second plank—the one that was closer to the hole—in order not to litter on it and subsequently direct our bottoms in the hole. Immediately after, we needed to spread our feet wide apart, bend our legs in half, lay our upper arms on our thighs to have stronger support over our bodies, and only then could we empty our bowels.

Perhaps to make me more comfortable, my father decided to build a toilet on which we could actually sit. Out of wood he made a rectangular box with an open top and bottom. Somehow he attached that box to the floor and the back wall of the outhouse. On top of it he nailed four more boards, two across and perpendicular, to make another rectangle; the hole in the middle served as a toilet bowl where our waste ran down into about a two-meter deep depression in the ground. I was often afraid that I would fall into that hole and get stuck in the smelly sewage.

On the front board across we could sit, and it was even polished with sandpaper and brushed with a yellowish lacquer. The other three were rough and not even touched by any kind of finish. Also two big nails did not totally penetrate the back part of the rectangle, and they remained about two inches higher above the boards. At first I thought that the protruding nails were meant for a newspaper to be hung on them, which served as our toilet paper. It could not have been so, though, because on both sides of the outhouse walls there were separate nails for that very purpose. On the left, there dangled, always upside-down, an old book, pierced with a three-inch nail by the hard front cover in the lower corner. The pages hung down loosely, separating themselves from each other, and it was easy to rip pages from it. We did not even need to wet our fingers with our saliva in order not to tear more than one page at the same time. On the right wall of the outhouse hung two or three old newspapers, folded in half, their corners, too, being folded up high in the air. One could really get enlightened by just spending a few hours a day inside it. Had it not been for the smell, the spiderwebs, and the dozens of flies flying above my head and below my feet, I would not have minded sitting there for hours, looking at the black and white pictures of our county's *inteligencia*. Politicians, doctors, and even General Secretary Brezhnev himself resided there, whose face I could recognize with my closed eyes anywhere, since his pictures almost never left our outhouse until about three months after his death in 1982.

Our outhouse was not a failure, though. At least it had a door; other people's did not. No mushrooms grew on its walls and floor, no leaking from its roof, and no loose pieces of slate hanging from the ceiling. One could jump and dance the Ukrainian *hopak* in our bathroom without shaking it. It never collapsed on anyone as our neighbor's did once while he was sitting on his toilet. He was totally buried by it, and my father and a few other neighbors had to rescue him. But it was not as if people were lazy or could not afford to build decent outhouses for themselves. It was just that the outhouses were not important in our village since people only spent a few minutes a day there.

I was perhaps the only one who sat there longer. Being a curious little girl, I liked to get up from our toilet, bend my head all the way down between my legs, and look at how and what was to come out of me. My mother often told me that if the food did not fit in my stomach, it would soon come outside. But instead of food, I often saw parasites coming out of there. Some were as long and fat as licorice strips. Seeing them, big tears would run down my cheeks, and I cried, hollering as loudly as I could until my father, who usually spent most of his time outside or in the stable around our animals, heard me and called my mother to come out and pull out my worms. Dropped into the dung, these too went into our wheat, potato, beet, and carrot fields to help them grow faster and bigger.

Nothing was ever wasted on our farm. Everybody's excrement—human, livestock, and even chicken waste, was collected for six months to be spread in the early spring and late fall on our fields. The fields had kept us—and many generations before us who had been responsible for turning forests into crop fields—alive. For that reason our outhouse was located right next to the piles of cow, horse, pig, and bird manure. All of them were mixed together so later they could enrich our soil.

Our dunghill was always so big that it was almost impossible to see the outhouse from behind it. The bigger the dunghill, the happier my father was, because it meant a bigger harvest. My father was so artistic in making a nice hill out of the dung that it looked exactly like the pyramids of Gaza. My father was a skillful farmer. He enjoyed

15

everything he did on his farm. Even when he dumped the animal manure on the hill, he did it with a joy and satisfaction. At first he would go around the stable, raking all the cow manure together in one corner, and repeated the same procedure with the rest of animals. Then little by little, with a shovel in his hands, he carried everything to the hill. He usually made about six or seven trips. Sometimes I heard him breathing hard, and once I saw sweat running down his right brow and landing on his cheek, which he managed to wipe it with his sleeve while carrying the dung to the dump. I can still see him raising a shovel to about the middle of his chest and drying his face with his smock-frock's sleeve.

After the stable was clean and all the manure was on the hill, he clapped his pyramid with a shovel several times to flatten it and make it smooth and glassy. It really was smooth and even glossy, especially when it was still fresh and damp. As it dried in the sun, it kept losing its shine, smell, and color all together to turn into dehydrated soil and looked pretty much like a wooden mulch. When it did not rain for a couple of weeks, the dung would become hard and almost stony. It was then that my younger brother Willy and a bunch of older kids used to make small tunnels through it. Once they managed to dig a big one. I, being ten years old at the time, could have freely crawled on my stomach through that tunnel without touching its walls with my clothes. But I never did because I was scared even to look at that tunnel. It reminded me of the burial plots in our local cemetery. I feared dead people, and I thought that the tunnel would devour me some day. I even envisioned ghosts and snakes being wrapped around my neck and biting me piece by piece.

My father was not happy about the tunnel. He thought it was unhealthy for my brother to dig into the manure and scared him that he too would get worms soon, just like me. Usually a few days after the tunnel would sink to the ground.

I was not happy about the dunghill. I feared that nobody would hear me from behind that hill when I screamed every time my parasites were coming out of me. My father always heard me, though. He knew why I was screaming. Everybody in our family and even a few next-door neighbors knew too. All of them were trying hard to help me. Once in a while two of the oldest ladies of the village—one in her eighties, the other way past ninety—used to come to our house to whisper something above my head. Had I not known that one was older than the other, I would never be able to tell the difference in their age. The older lady was about five feet tall. She certainly must have been taller in her younger days, but at the present time a big hump on her back prevented her from standing straight. When I was about five, I asked her: "Lady Martina, why do you carry a bowl on your back?"

"Where?" she asked.

"Under your shirt! There!" I said, pointing my index finger to her hump.

"Oh-h. That's not a bowl, that's a sack where I hide all bad children. Two of them are sitting there right now. Do you wanna touch it?" she said, turning her back to me and bending over even further so I could reach it. I did not want to put my hand there, though; I envisioned the two poor kids bound in the dark with a rope.

Four years later, at the time she was working on my worms, the hump was even bigger. Her body was rounded, and it looked like a letter "C," with her head and feet slanted forward, but her bust arched like a crescent moon. That hunch perhaps made thirty percent of her weight, but even with it she could not have been more than eighty-five pounds. There was nothing on her body but skin and bones.

The younger one, Lady Paraska, did not have a hump; yet, she too was slim, much taller, though, about five foot six inches. Her face and hands had thousands of wrinkles, and because of them she looked older than Lady Martina. Her head was bundled in the kerchief, with its ends double knotted on the back of her neck. She pretty much looked like the victim of the Stalinist holocaust. It's not as if she was poor and did not have anything to eat. Nobody starved in our village, at least in my time; it was just that she did not have any molars left to chew her food with. She still had three teeth in front, two on top, and one on the bottom, but even those were just about to fall out. Two of them kept moving, going back and forth, every time she touched them with her bottom lip while talking.

When they were whispering, I had to kneel on the floor on my skinny knees so they could remove all kinds of freeloaders from inside my body. They always mumbled at the same time, each saying her own incantation, and I was wondering what would happen had the ladies mixed the words of their petitions. They talked so fast that their language was almost foreign to me. One was definitely praying because she must have mentioned the word of Saint Katharine a dozen times; I heard the other declaring, "You are not allowed to be neither in the left nor in the right, neither in on top nor in the bottom, neither in the belly nor in the liver, nowhere in that small child's body." I did not know who she meant by "you," but I guess that was how she addressed my worms. While whispering, the ladies kept looking, not at me, but into a two-handled cup of water that each held with one hand above my head. When I tried to elevate my head to look at them, both quickly gave me a small smack on the back of my head to return to the previous position. Soon they too switched their position and one stood in front of me, the other behind my back; I did not know whether it was part of the procedure or because I interfered by sticking my head into their secrets.

They whispered for about ten minutes, then the oldest lady made a big cross on my head with a small kitchen knife while the younger one made another cross on the cup. Only then did they let me get up and take three small sips of water from the cup. With the rest of it both washed my face, stomach, hands, and even feet, one taking responsibility on the left, the other on the right. What was left in the cup was given to my mother to dump on our dunghill. The oldest lady gave my mother special instructions on how to discard the rest of the water on the dump. She had to face back the dunghill, take the cup into her right hand, spill the water over her left shoulder, and leave the cup by the threshold for them to pick up on the way out. It was crucial for her to do exactly what she was told; otherwise, the matrons' time would be wasted.

I believed in the ladies Martina and Paraska; I knew that those whispering dames were trying to make me healthy. But I liked it better when my mother took care of me, and when she did her own magic on me, which was not as intense as the ladies'. She prayed a little, and then took nine of my fingers into her hands and put each of them into her mouth one by one, starting from the thumb. She sucked on each fingertip gently for less than a second, and made it seem as if she was spitting to the ground. There was no spit, though, I only heard her saying "Phy." And then she would hug me and kiss my hair. I once asked her, "Mama, why do you only suck nine of my fingers, why do you leave out the little one on the left?" She did not exactly know the answer to that. It had to do something with nine saintly people, and that was how her mother, my grandmother whom I never met, had taught her. I liked that my mother was always the first one who came to my rescue.

Always keeping the door of the outhouse open, I enjoyed seeing her running towards me, wiping her hands in her apron because they were either wet or greasy from the kitchen work. She was always the one who did the dirty work for me and made me feel better. Immediately after she took care of me, I would promise myself not to eat wormy apples anymore. But after a week or so I kept breaking my own promise. I do not know whether it was the apples' redness, their enormous size, or both that kept seducing and conquering me to their side. I just could not overcome my addiction to them. Apples were my weakness; I liked them better than our famous delicacy candies—sweet tootsie rolls.

***

For a long time nobody knew why I always had intestinal worms. It was not unusual for a six-year-old or a younger child in our village to have worms, but I had long passed that age. I was nine, and my mother now needed to pray longer and do even more than that. A nurse used to come to our house once a week to measure my temperature and give me two pills. One tasted like over-salted pickled cabbage; the other like a spoiled egg. Both made me throw up. Then she used to come every day for two weeks to inject my bottom with needles. She assured my parents that the intestinal worms were not a serious problem, that it was a part of a child growing up. She even named a few kids, now grown-ups, who had gone through similar problems and turned out just fine. Perhaps she was right because as soon as I reached puberty, my worms left me forever.

After the injections the worms vanished for a while too; a few months later they were back. But every time my worms disappeared, my mother could not thank enough the two whispering ladies because she did not as much trust the medicine as them. For the entire month she prayed every day for them to live many years and asked me to do the same. She went to their houses and for another month kept bringing them eggs, cheese, and sour cream. When the fall came, she was always the first one to dig out their potatoes. In the winter she remembered to deliver them milk even though there was not enough of it for us, the children, much less her and my father, since our cows barely milked during that time because they were getting ready to have calves. Before Christmas she brought them pig's liver, bacon, and lard because it was during that time that we used to slaughter the biggest, fattest pig so we could have fresh meat for the holidays.

Those were the best times even though it was not pleasant to hear and see what the poor pig had to go through to end up on our table. No matter whether I buried my head into the pillow or hid myself under the bed, I could still hear the squeals of the pig and the pigs of half of our village. Everybody's families slaughtered their pigs a few weeks before Christmas. Sometimes six or seven were slaughtered on the same day, and there was a reason why. Since people fasted before Christmas, pigs could only be butchered three times a week—Tuesday, Thursday, or Saturday. On those days we were allowed to have some meat. On Sunday too. But since Sunday was God's day, people could not kill on that day.

Six strong men were in command of one pig. At first it had to be knocked to the ground and laid on its right side. Two men, kneeling on the pig's abdomen, held its front legs, tied with a silk rope. The other two captured the back ones, sitting on the pig's thighs. The fifth man grabbed the ears and nostrils, lying on its neck while the last one was responsible for finding its heart with a twenty-inch knife. If he could not, that pig and all of the men were in trouble because the pig often went wild and managed to release itself from the rope and attacked each man separately, biting their hands, feet, and even faces. After that another five or six men had to be called to catch, maintain, and finally subdue one big, fat, angry pig.

When I no longer heard the squeals, I knew I could get out from under the bed. It was also time for my mother to go outside and place a ten-liter basin under the pig's heart for its blood to flow into because later that blood, cooked and mixed with rice, garlic, onion, pepper, and salt and stuffed into the pig's small intestines, would serve as our sausage.

Outside I saw blood running down the pig's gut. At first it poured into the basin. Five minutes later it slowly streamed and then dripped there. As time went by, only a small amount of blood would drop again into the basin, usually when someone accidentally poked the pig in the stomach with a boot.

The blood was everywhere: on men's hands, clothes, faces, the handle of a knife, which lay on the ground by the pig's front legs. Five feet of snow, where the animal rested, looked like Santa's robe. When there was no more blood coming out, two six-inch steel hooks would be hammered into the pig's back legs.

The day before, four sharp-edged pointed wooden poles—paired—were drilled into the frozen ground. Each pair was crisscrossed, struck with a fat nail, which looked more like a bolt, and wrapped around with a rope about five times on every angle. Equipped, they were positioned about seven feet apart. On top, there stood a horizontal steel bar. The same six men, some holding the pig's rump, others the backbone, and the rest the head, lifted the pig and hung it upside down on the bar by the hooks bayoneted into its legs. To get rid of the animal's hair, one man immediately started burning the entire pig with a torch until it acquired a coal-mine color. After the desired hue was achieved, my father poured two buckets of boiling water over it so it would be easy to peel the charred surface with a blade. When the outer skin came off, the pig's flesh had the gentle pale color of an infant child, not a single hair on it.

Now the pig was ready to be butchered. At first it was beheaded—by the same man who stabbed it in the heart. The head came off as easily as if he was cutting a watermelon in half. Immediately after my mother again placed a basin under its body to get more blood. My father took the head in his hands and hid it in the snow so the dogs would not eat it. When the basin was taken away, one man started carving the pig piece by piece until there were nothing but ribs and guts. Heart, liver, and spleen were taken out at the very end and handed to my mother to be cooked immediately because those six men would later be invited to our house for vodka and meat, which was part of our gratitude for the people who had helped us to slaughter the pig.

Some of the cuts of meat were about three to four feet long; two men had to carry them on our porch and lay them on the table and even on the floor if there was no more room there. The top pieces, though, did not contain any meat; they were all fat, some about four inches thick. A lot of fat always made our family happy because there would be so many things we could do with it. Some was chopped into tiny pieces by my mother—who was our chopping master—to be melted in the oven, filtered through a gauze, and cooled down so we could have enough lard until the next Christmas.

My father was responsible for the thickest pieces of fat. Those he usually cut into twelve-inch squares, and arranged them in a wooden box. He usually fitted five layers in that box. On the bottom of the box he placed a cloth completely buried in salt. It was almost as if he was making lasagna or a layer cake. After each layer, he spread over about an inch-thick amount of salt. A few months later we would have to scrape off that salt every time we were ready to consume our raw lard. But in the meantime my father submerged his final layer into salt, placed another cloth on the top of it, hammered the box with a nail, and carried it to our underground basement, where we maintained all of our preserved food, even potatoes. The basement also served as our refrigerator in the summer. Since we could not preserve fresh meat there in the summer, my mother cut all the meat into small pieces, mixed it with a lot of salt too, and put it in three-liter glass jars. Those too went to the basement.

A lot of food could be preserved in our basement during the summer. The dairy products could not. Butter gave us the most trouble, but we found a solution for that too. There was a seven-meter well, our drinking water, in our back yard, which had been dug by my great grandfather. The water there was ice cold even during the hottest summer days. We used to put the butter in a small sealed bowl and place the bowl in a pail half filled with water. On the rope we lowered the pail into the well, and that way we were able to keep the butter for more than a week. But every time we needed to use butter, we had to go to the well. There was this popular slogan in our village, "Wanna butter, go to the well." Sometimes pieces of chicken, duck, turkey, or goose, and leftover jars of salted pig would abide there for a few days too.

Preserved pig usually lasted until June. Therefore, during the winter we rushed to use it to make conserved meat, *pashtets*, and smoked-dried kielbasas. It took my parents about two weeks to put the pig in the jars, boxes, and containers.

I never wanted to see our pig being slaughtered, but I liked to eat it, especially when my mother would fry me liver with garlic and onion, which was my favorite. I did not even want to share it with my brother; I wrinkled my nose, knitted my brow, and bit my tongue when she took a few pieces out of the casserole and put them into two bowls for me to deliver to Martina and Paraska. If I told her I did not want to share my liver with the two ladies, she would immediately reply: "Don't you remember the summer? They made your worms go away. You oughta share some with them!" And so I did.

***

As soon as all the snow melted on our streets, as soon as the sun warmed up our ground, and as soon as I was able to run barefoot in our yard, my worms were back. And again the whispering ladies and the nurse had to be invited to our house. One summer day my father concluded that my worms were the result of my eating unripe wormy apples. More than that, he caught me throwing rocks at one of the apple trees. He did not spank me; he never did. He just told me that those big rocks would hurt the apple tree, and we would not be able to have apples the next year. I felt bad for those trees. I often prayed to God to forgive me for hurting them and let us have apples again the next year. In exchange for apples, I promised Him to go to church every Sunday and try not to chat and giggle with my friends during the Holy Liturgy. I was a sensitive and conscientious child. Had my father known that, perhaps he would have explained more things to me—why he did not care about the story of my birth, and why he never played with me. I wanted him to open his heart for me; he never did.

Sometimes it seemed he not only closed his heart but also did not wish to bother with me, even at the times when I displayed inappropriate conduct. When my mother expressed her concerns that I misbehaved in church, he did not yell at me. Other kids would either be smacked on their heads, receive ten belt lashes on their bottoms, forced to kneel in the corner with their hands raised in the air for half an hour, or be compelled to scrub hen coops for three days. I was never punished. He waved his hand in my mother's direction, said, "Eh-h," and went outside to his stable.

Perhaps I got off so easily because he never went to church. Not that he did not believe in God. He was a believer, and he was faithful to God, Jesus, and the Virgin Mary. I personally saw him praying every night. There was not a single day that he would miss his prayer. Even when he was drunk, which happened during weddings and christenings, he never forgot to pray. I saw him praying once during one of those drunken nights. He was kneeling on the floor before his bed for a long time, whispering his prayers, and then I saw his head falling on the pillow. My mother came and tried to wake him up, but she could not. He started to mumble his prayers again, but did not wake up. So, she put her hands under his armpits, raised his chest a little to put it across the bed. Then she did the same with his feet, and without taking off his shoes let him sleep. Even in bed, he was still mumbling his prayer. His prayers were usually short, five minutes or less, but on his drunken nights they lasted for hours.

Even though he was a true follower of Christ, my mother could never make my father go to church or to confession. She went to confession every month. He went once, the day before his wedding; otherwise, the priest and my grandma would not have let him marry my mother. He would constantly say to my mother that he would rather tell his sins to her than to those government-appointed priests.

"God knows my sins. Why do I need to say them to that communist, to that father, terrible Ivan?" he conveyed to her.

My mother would cover her mouth with both of her hands, look at her favorite icon of the Virgin Mary, and say, "Oh Mary of God." She was ashamed for him, and she had to pray even longer and confess not only for her but for his sins as well. I doubt whether she disclosed to preacher Ivan that my father called him a communist and Ivan the Terrible because he never received a letter to appear at our county's police station.

Maybe because my father disagreed with the communists monitoring our church, he never went to pray there and never yelled at me when he learned that I had giggled during the ceremony. But otherwise, he demanded a lot from me, more than anybody else in our village, more than my mother ever did. Unlike my mother, he made me do my homework and would not let me play until I showed it to him. When I made a hole in my notebook while in first grade because I was trying to erase an incorrectly spelled word written in blue ink, he ordered me to rewrite the whole sentence on a new page.

He was pretty knowledgeable on all school matters because he was one of the few people in our village who had graduated from high school. Unlike others, he had gone to school for eight years. He had also spent three years in the military and received an additional two years of educational training there. At one point he even dreamed of going to vocational school. His father died fairly early, though; circumstances forced him to quickly relinquish his dream and instead become a provider for his five younger brothers and sisters. So, my father knew something about education. And when I earned only three points in calligraphy, equal to an American C, in the second grade, he told me that not only would I never become a sales clerk in our local supermarket, which was my favorite profession until the fourth grade because I thought I could eat as much candies as I wanted, but I would have to twirl horses' tails for a living.

That was the biggest insult a child could get from a parent in our village. Nobody wanted to twirl horses' tails. Many parents scared their children about that profession to improve their grades, and it worked. After the insult their grades would significantly improve and remain improved for several months. Only one person in our village did not mind twirling horses' tails—old Peter "the brainless." He could not write or read, never went to school, nobody remembered his parents; he never had a wife or kids of his own, and was neither informed of nor invited to participate in the public gatherings of our village or in the local elections, even though those were mandatory for everybody. But there was something special about him. He liked animals and worked for our kolkhoz, a joint collective farm, as a stylist for horses' tails.

Not all land was collective, though. Every family in our village had ten to fifteen acres of their own land; the rest, about 300 acres, belonged to our kolkhoz. For one thing we were the luckiest people in the Soviet Union because Stalin had not had a chance to seize all of our property since it was not until 1939 that we became part of the great empire. When World War II started, our generalissimo father did not have time to hassle with our unfertile land. He had more important things to do. But even after the war was long over, only seven people from our village were completely deprived of their land and sent to Siberia. Two of them just had to be shipped there because they held too much control over our village; they co-owned our mill. A week after the two men left our village, the mill was demolished by a bulldozer. As a result, we had to ride horses for fifty kilometers to grind our wheat.

The owners of our supermarket and school were declared our enemies too; luckily their buildings were not destroyed. The buildings were granted to us by the mayor of our province who personally arrived in our village to read a long speech about the foes of our new country. At the end of his speech he cheered us up and declared that we no longer needed to depend on one person for goods or pay someone to go to school, but from now on we would be in possession of both the supermarket and the school. The applause lasted for more than two minutes. But as the two men were saying goodbye, the same people who applauded the mayor now wiped their tears and hid their faces in their collars so watchmen would not detect that they pitied the bourgeois. The memory of the two men would stay with us forever, though, every time we looked at our school and supermarket, constructed by their own naked hands, with help from nothing else besides saws and axes. Every time we filled our pockets and grocery bags with food or took our kids to school on their first day, we knew whom should we be thankful for. Had those buildings been bulldozed, just like our mill, we perhaps never would have obtained another supermarket or school. To this day our village is mill free.

The last person, an owner of a library, was the most dangerous to our village since he possessed too many books, written in our national language. More than that, he forgot to destroy our "nationalistic" blue and yellow flag, which stood for our independence. Once the flag was found behind the bookshelves, there was nothing the librarian could have done to save himself from the Gulag, even if he had placed fifty hammers and sickles and red flags in every window and all around the building. The library too was not destroyed. It was locked for about two years; its doors and window were nailed with plywood. Later the old books were replaced with new ones, and only then the library became the property of our village.

So, we only had a few enemies, and about two or three of the other men were labeled as kulaks. They too were sent somewhere; nobody knew where, though. At one time Peter boasted he knew where they were, but nobody took him seriously. The village people thought he was too dumb to have such information; after a while Peter stopped talking about it. He just listened, not only to the conversations of our village people but to the authority as well. He had a close association with the authority since he braided their horses. They spoke freely in front of Peter and acted as if he did not exist. They thought higher about their horses than about Peter. But Peter kept on listening, at the same time maintaining his quality work and being a dedicated kolkhoz worker. Many of his horses had braided tails. Some were spiral and tied up with red, black, and white ribbons. The horses' tails looked cute, like those one can often see in the international horse race competitions. For as little as a few pennies, Peter could texture anyone's horse. For that reason not only the collective but almost all private farmers' horses were twined as well. Our horse was not; I do not know why to this day.

But there was one problem. Peter was getting old and weak, and there was no one to replace him. That profession was not respected in our village because people did not have a favorable opinion about Peter not being able to read and write. On Sunday after church people usually gathered in front of our supermarket to discuss the latest news. A mailman used to come out on the street at that very moment because it was a good time for him to deliver newspapers to everybody at once without having to go to each house separately later. He passed the newspaper to every man. Each one of them without even looking at it rolled the newspaper in a tube and put it in the back pocket of his pants. Peter, who sat on the edge of the bench all alone, with his hat pulled over his eyes, with his hands clutched on his stomach, and with his feet hidden under the seat, was the only man who did not get a newspaper. Seeing him like that, the fourth graders, three or four of them, quickly grabbed the newspapers from their parents' pockets, held them before Peter's eyes, and demanded that he read the main titles. He joked at first by making up silly names, and all kids would be holding their bellies from laughs. The parents ignored the whole scene since their kids had a good time, and nobody was torturing them. Then Peter would get up from the bench and slowly walked home without saying goodbye to anyone. Nobody, the children in particular, wanted to be like Peter because they thought that he was not even good enough to face the horse. He was only good at facing horses' tails. They felt that tails were the reason why Peter could not identify the titles of the newspapers. By twining horses tails, they too would not be able to read and write and lose their brain just as Peter had. Therefore, every time the children did badly in school, their parents threatened them with Peter the brainless' profession.

When my father told me that I would replace Peter and take over his career, I was wounded. I cried because I did not like that profession even though I adored horses. But most of all I could not accept my father's treating me as if I was not a special child, as if I was like the rest of the village's kids. It was then that I seriously started to think about my homework, and by the forth grade I had finally earned my very first "5" in math, the highest grade, equal to an A.

My father remained unimpressed. He continued to take me on our usual trips to the supermarket but bought me no extra candy or anything like that. He never hugged me and did not give me any reason to hug him either. He never called me his princess—like a few other intellectual fathers I knew, one of whom was the head of our kolkhoz, the other a bookkeeper, the last the principal of our school—even though I was, according to the village people, an adorable child, with chubby cheeks, button nose, summer sky-blue eyes, long dark eyelashes and eyebrows, and curly blonde hair. I even acquired the nickname: "Baby-Doll." Way past twelve, people still called me Baby-Doll, except my father. He was the only person who never called me by a nickname, except Anita or once in a while Anitochka. I knew he loved me according to his bond, but I did not feel that I was his special girl.

In revenge, I would not give him a hug before going to bed. When my mother told me my story at bedtime, I imagined myself being a "big person," exactly like our local librarian, tall, with my hair cut short like hers since every other woman in our village had long hair, plaited in Amish style. I imagined myself without a kerchief on my head and no apron around my waist. One time my father interrupted my dreams and said to my mother, whispering into her ear, thinking I was asleep: "I don't know, the way you spoil her, she'll never be anything." After that I constantly closed my eyes, pretending I was sleeping, every time he walked inside my room at night, and every time my mother asked me to say a little prayer to keep our daddy healthy and strong. But I prayed to God to give me a better father, instead. In my view there was nothing special about him: reddish potato nose, big bags around his eyes, long gray hair combed backwards from his forehead all the way to his neck. Yet, two tiny locks of his hair were never able to stay back, and they always hung over his forehead. Some hair peeped from his ears and nose, and two small ones from his right cheek, very close to his eye. His blue eyes were perhaps the most attractive feature of his appearance. I got mine from him. They were so clear and wide open that even when he was angry, no one could see the anger in his eyes. But his blue eyes were not enough for me, and he was not going to buy my love with them.

I just knew that my relationship with my father was not anything like my friends'. It seemed to me that our love was not even true in comparison with the stories of father-daughter relationships that I observed on our librarian's television. Those other fathers would hold their daughters on their laps, hugging, kissing, and playing soccer or other kids' games with them; but my father never hugged me, never played soccer with me, and never bought me any toy. Instead of toys, I played with wrapping paper, left over from tootsie rolls, rocks I collected from our five-foot-wide two-foot deep stream—which was called a river and was even marked on the map—where even one-inch fish and frogs had a hard time making a decent living, and wood sticks left over from firewood that my father cut with a handsaw and then chopped with an axe to prepare for winter. Sometimes, when I agreed to help him to carry a few logs to the shed, where we made a wall out of them, he took one log in his hand and cleaved a few pieces, as thin as a ruler, for me to play with. But I wanted to have a doll, like the principal's daughter. I never got one. Instead, when I was about nine, he got me a green hair clip. The hair clip was not even a toy, but it was the only thing I remember he ever gave me. I kept it in my closet for more than five years until my brother laid his hands on it and broke it into two pieces.

Perhaps had I not had a younger brother, my relationship with my father might have been much different. Once that little big-nosed goblin was born, all his attention from me switched to that boy. I had to share everything with him, even my room and often my bed, when he was scared to sleep by himself. My father expected me to teach him how to tie his shoes. I had to clean him up when he fell in a puddle. My father and I had our casual trips to the supermarket—located about a thousand feet from our house—only when my brother was chasing grasshoppers or dissecting bugs and did not see us; the three of us had to go together most of the time. But worse than that, it appeared to me that after all I had done for my brother, my father was still much friendlier to him than to me. When I was about ten, I watched my father schooling my five-year-old brother on how to ride a horse. My brother constantly cried because he was afraid of horses, and it took my father several years to coax him onto the horse and get him to hold on to it without anyone's supervision. I always laughed at my brother, and I usually ran after my father, screaming, "Daddy, Daddy, I'm not afraid. I wanna do it. I wanna do it." He let me sit on a horse for a few minutes but instead of praising me for bravery, he would say, "Why, you don't need to do that! Horses are not for girls. You ought to get away from them as far as you can, and you will some day. You're too gentle for a horse." But even if he thought that I was too gentle, he never showed me that I was. How could I have known back then that it was my father's dream to get me away from both, the horses and his way of life?

As I became older, I depended less and less on him. I was my own person. I did not care any more whether he loved my brother more than me. Although I did reconcile myself to my brother soon after. At fourteen, I was still at that stage when it was better for a girl not to get into the boy crowd. Once I did. About six boys, some younger, some older, and some my age, made a ring around me and called me "shred butt." There was a reason for that name. Back in sixth grade, while I was trying to run away from our rooster, I landed on the piece of barbed wire. Both my underwear and my butt got ripped. A few boys saw my bloody underwear; since that day I was shred butt. Now they would not leave me alone. My brother was there too, and I was just waiting for him to call me that name so I could later bite his ears and break his head. He always hung out with the older crowd because they taught him how to smoke and helped him torture frogs, fish, and miniature crabs. At home he called me shred butt almost every day, and there was not a single day that I did not lock him in the horse stable for that. But to my surprise he was silent now. Their leader saw that and instantly commanded: "Tell her to show us her butt." My brother put his hands in his pocket, looked into the ground, and started to make circles with his right shoe.

"Tell her, I'll give you two cigarettes…. Let you hold my frogs for the whole week," he said.

My brother took out one hand from his pocket, slowly dragged himself into the ring where I stood, and still observing the ground said, "Wanna go home?" We did go home together, holding our hands, but neither of us said a word to each other. I did not let go of his hand until I turned the knob of our door because I did not want my father and particularly my mother to have a heart attack. There was a better chance for them to accept the rumor that their worst enemy Stalin had risen from death than seeing me holding my brother's hand. I myself felt uncomfortable, and for that reason I walked silently and awkwardly as if I had pooped in my pants. It was not until the tenth grade that I was not embarrassed any more to hug him once in a while in front of my parents. But after that day I knew I could use a brother. During my high school years he was my best informer as to whether my boyfriends had any other girlfriends besides me.

***

I had suddenly discovered a use for my brother, but I thought I could perfectly survive without my father. I had my own life with many friends, and my mother seemed to be on my side because she was the one who always talked to him every time I needed money to buy new clothes or my favorite lingerie items. He was in control of our finances, but I have to say that he was not some control freak. Everybody, even I, knew that our savings always stayed in the same place—in the coffee mug in the kitchen cabinet. We just needed to let him know when and why the money needed to be used.

He had no problem in letting me take some money out of the mug for school lunches or my favorite candies that I could now buy myself without asking him to go with me. Now I liked to go with my girlfriends because we could enjoy eating them all together and have our regular competition as to who would finish their candies first. The person who finished last had to buy more candies and share equally with the rest. If there was a single piece, we each bit a piece from it, trying to be fair to one another. Often it was hard to bite it, so we sucked on it, licking three times, until the oldest of us was finally able to break it into small pieces with her front teeth and hand each one of us a separate chunk, which was the best because we did not need to take it out of our mouths and share it with others any longer. I often ended up eating my candies last, so I needed to buy more. I knew I would not be able to take more money out of the coffee mug; luckily our supermarket accepted chicken eggs. One egg counted as six pennies; with two of them I could buy one hundred grams worth, six or seven tootsie rolls or other caramel candies.

Our chickens laid eggs everywhere they could find stacks of dried hay. I discovered some places with eggs my father and mother never even knew about. So I had no problem in buying more candies. The only problem was that the sales clerk often asked whether our parents knew about our bringing eggs to the store. When she asked me that question, I nodded my head yes without worrying that she would later ask my father whether he had really let me have the eggs. But for two eggs she usually did not bother to make such an inquiry; three or more meant trouble because she made certain that our parents knew about it. If she found out that the eggs were stolen, that child could not bring eggs to the supermarket for a few months. Only when the clerk would forget about it or at the time when our supermarket was full of people on the days when fresh bread was delivered to our village by a lorry, which pretty much looked like a nineteen-foot U-Haul truck, could she have accepted the eggs from that child because she did not have time to think about them.

When a white truck drove through our village every Friday after lunchtime, everybody knew it was time to leave the field, kitchen, or stable work and hurry to the store. Before even seeing the truck, people ran there to form a line because everybody wanted to be first. The whole village knew the loud scraping sound of an approaching truck, and it could be heard from about a mile away. On some days the bread truck was the only vehicle that ran on the street of our village in a twenty-four-hour period. Not many people wanted to drive to our village with their automobiles. We were lucky to get the bread truck, and it only came because its owner was required to do so by the county. But the driver was not happy at all because often his truck got stuck in one of our road's four-foot-wide craters and could not get out until several strong men had helped him. The driver had to go from door to door asking for help, but the village cooperated quickly. After a while he did not even have to call anybody because once we kids heard the truck's loud noise, we ran home to call our fathers to come out into the street to help the bread truck to get to the supermarket. Our fathers pushed it with their backs, hands, and some with wooden sticks or steel rods until it finally made it out of the hole. At the end everybody cheered, and it was a good occasion for those men to get together in the evening on that very day and have a glass of vodka with a snack of green leaves of garlic and onion.

We children knew that it was a good time for us to buy candy on bread day. The supermarket was filled with people; some had to stay outside because there was no room inside. In such an environment the clerk whose name was Mary could never remember the stolen eggs at the time when other people were disputing why one person would get to buy six loaves of bread but the another only four. Mary was pretty fair, but people still gave her trouble even though she was a masculine woman who could have easily overpowered any woman and about half of our short village men because of her unusual height—she was about a foot taller than the average man and almost twice the size of my father. She was a lively forty-five-year-old woman with brown hair and a half-inch shamrock birthmark above her left eyebrow, which was another distinctive feature of her appearance. Mary never used her strength on people; though it would not have surprised me a bit if she had done that during bread time. She allowed those with a family of six or more to obtain six loaves of bread, each of which cost exactly one ruble; those with fewer, only four. She announced that at the very beginning, before the bread was even unloaded from the truck. Every time a person with a small family held six loaves in his or her hand, he was asked to put two back. Before putting them back, he asked the same question over and over again, "Why?" She again had to give the same answer to every such person: that only those with six or more could have more bread because the truck was not fully loaded.

For us it was the best time to bring eggs. At the moment when other people were quarreling over who got how many loaves of bread and how many times they should stay in line, thinking she would not remember them, we would stick our eggs before her face with our guilty expressions and ask her for candy. It was not the time for candies during bread time, but she still let us have them sometimes. Often she hollered at us to come back later because candy was not important. But when she was too exhausted from trying to outshout about fifty people talking at the same time, she just grabbed the eggs from our hands without ever realizing what she was doing and threw six candies straight at us or into our pockets, forgetting to put them on the scale first and then make a funnel from a newspaper to be able to drop them inside.

She was skillful in making paper funnels; I was never able to do it as well as she did no matter how many times I practiced it at home or while sitting in our outhouse. She would roll the paper to make a tube, frizzled up its end to keep the funnel from loosening, and then slide the candies into it with her palm. When the candies were inside, she closed the funnel so our candies would stay in one place without being lost on the way out. It was kind of sad when she did not make the funnel for us. Many times, during bread times, she gave us the wrong candies, but we were happy because she often fetched us more expensive ones. One of my girlfriends even got chocolates once.

I never got the chocolates, but I felt I was walking on air when after showing my eggs to her, she let me put them in the paper box. Several times, seeing my eggs, she rolled her eyes but pointed her hand at the egg box without even looking directly at me; she would be arguing with those customers who held a mountain of bread in their arms, all the way up to their chins, which frequently covered their shoulders and necks. Our bread looked pretty much like a brownish brick—all the same and as monotonous as the rest of our country's planned economy. Each loaf was fifteen-by-seven inches and weighed about four pounds. But I did not care about the bread; I enjoyed putting eggs in the box because I felt as if I was performing a clerk's duties. After the eggs were in the box, I would pull her sleeve to let her know that my job was done and I needed to get paid. But, instead, she asked: "What do you want?"

I pointed at the tootsie rolls, and she, to get rid of me, would wave her hand at me saying, "Just get it yourself," which made me even more happy.

And I, hesitating, would ask another question, "Should I take six or seven?"

"Seven is fine," she grumbled and continued to argue with the customers who stood in the line for the second time. She repeated over and over again: "People, do not bother to even come close to me for the second time until everybody gets their share."

Then a few would scream: "Everybody's been here already. It's time for the second round."

And she would answer, "Don't you people understand that some still work in the fields, and they couldn't get here as fast as you, Peter? Go home and come back later. If there are leftovers, I won't take them home with me. I'll let you have more later," she lectured them.

It was as if she was conversing with a bunch of deaf people because they did not even move. She had to embarrass everyone, who tried to trick her, separately. When my sixty-two-year-old aunt, my father's eldest sister, stood there for the second time—and she did it constantly—the clerk would scream at her: "Mrs. Shyshak, you just bought your bread twenty minutes ago! What are you doing here?"

My aunt, a short and nimble white-headed woman, without even blushing, would utter with authority: "I'm not buying for myself but for my brother."

The clerk would say, "But your brother bought his bread already too."

"Oh. I didn't know that," she said.

"He was standing next to you," the clerk would say, and only then would my aunt leave the line—but not the store.

My father usually waited outside to get his second chance. And because he never argued with the clerk, he was the first one to receive the leftovers. Sometimes when he noticed me in the crowd, he would hand me some pennies without my asking him for them. But even if I did, he would not have said no because it was not customary to refuse a child in a crowd, particularly on Friday.

***

Up to my teen years, he rarely refused to give me some money for delicacies and my favorite books. But when I was fifteen, I needed to buy lipstick and mascara. For those I had to ask my mother. He used to say to me that he would never deny me money for food because eating

35

well was important.

"The poison," as he referred to lipsticks, "that she puts on her lips is not worth money," he used to say to my mother when she begged him to give me money because I needed to be like everyone else. Sometimes I would hear her telling him that all girls at this age use these things and that I needed not to be behind. No one could persuade him otherwise, and I had to sacrifice my lunch money to buy these girl things. Of course, that poison was not available in our supermarket, but we found our way to compete with the rest of the modern world and acquire a city look. Our city girl Katarina supplied us with it. She was not really a city girl; she only worked there as a cashier for our county's only gas station. We thought Katarina was an important person, and we were sad and at the same time envious to see her leaving our village every Monday morning because we could not go with her. But we were always happy to meet her every Friday night by our supermarket because she brought us our goods. Sometimes all of her pockets were full of our lipstick, mascara, and nail polish, and she made a ruble on each item she sold. So I was angry at my father that I did not have school lunches for weeks, sometimes months. I thought he was heartless and so stupid not to understand that I lived in the eighties and not the tsarist feudal period.

It was then that I started to notice one thing about him that annoyed me the most—his teeth. I could have forgiven him for not teaching me how to ride a horse, not understanding that I was a girl and had to compete with my classmates, and even for not paying any attention to the story of my birth. I could not forgive him, though, for his teeth. It was even embarrassing for me to talk to other people about his teeth. I only talked about it with my best friend, Hana, who was one year younger than I. I felt unfortunate that we were not in the same classroom, and once, when I was eight, I had a wishful thought that I should just stay in the same grade for another year. As I spoke my dream aloud, my father dispelled that idea quickly from my head by telling me that maybe I should not go to school at all but instead milk our cows.

But as soon as the school bell rang, Hana and I left our seats and dashed outside to be with each other. Hana was a true friend. She was about ten pounds overweight, and kids used to call her "fat potato pancake." Though her mother did not believe so. If Hana did not take her potato pancakes to school for lunch, her mother bundled them in the notebook and then in a newspaper and ran after her hollering: "You forgot your lunch again, Hana! Look at you! Skinny as a stick!" Her face was slim, but she was never skinny. That made all kids fifty feet ahead turn their heads around and laugh, even me because I did not know how could she think that Hana was skinny. I could say I was the skinniest out of all.

Hana would hide the lunch in her pocket looking to the side and continue walking, not even waiting for me and not noticing that I was five feet behind. Both of us felt that we had a lot in common. She had her mother; I—my father's teeth. Once I laughed about my father, confiding to Hana that if there were annual awards for people with the worst teeth, my father would have gotten one every year.

There was probably not a single person in the entire world who could compete with him in that. My father's teeth were not even mustard yellow, they bore the mildew's bloom of three-month-old bread that almost everybody, at least once in a lifetime, finds in their kitchen. I knew that nobody over forty or below seven brushed their teeth in our village. I was seven the first time I started to brush mine. My first teacher, who was about twenty, told all of us in class that if we wanted our teeth to be healthy, we needed to brush them at least twice a day. It seemed weird at first. But since she was the only girl in the village who had straight white teeth—everybody could figure out she was not from our village—I decided to trust her. She even told us that everybody had to have their own toothbrush, which was totally absurd to me. For a long time I could not understand how the world could afford to make toothbrushes for everyone. Still, I was impressed with my teacher, and I immediately wanted to be as clean as she was because her clothes smelled fresh. I never smelled garlic or onion on her. Her outfits did not have grease spots around her belly either. Though, I decided that I would share my toothbrush with my entire family. But since no one in my family was the right age for a toothbrush, it was all mine. And I got it because of the great generosity of our government who distributed toothbrushes to every first grader for free, which I kept for five years until they finally started to be available in our supermarket. Had my father gotten his toothbrush for free in his first grade, perhaps he too might have brushed them.

It was not as though my father forgot about his teeth; quite the opposite was true. He was more aware of his teeth than the rest of those around him; it was just that he did not believe in the word "toothbrush." Other people in the village did not believe in it either, but somehow they managed to have quite acceptable teeth, much better than my father's. Half of the village, though, got rid of their front teeth and replaced them with metal ones; their teeth looked almost like Jaws' from the *Bond* films. Even now, every time I watch *The Spy Who Loved Me* and see Jaws' smile, I think about my village.

Metal teeth were popular in my village. They lasted almost for life. They were convenient and practical, and people could bite anything with them, even chicken bones. They could chew the biggest pieces of pig skin with them too. So they just had to take some time off from their busy schedules and traveled fifty kilometers away from our village to get their metal teeth.

At one point of our history, metal teeth were fashionable not only in our village, but in the city, too and throughout the entire Soviet Union—not steel teeth, though, but the gold ones. Especially high-class people were almost psychotic about the gold teeth; some pulled out their healthy teeth on purpose so they could obtain a golden smile. My Uncle Stephen got rid of his molars entirely and covered his healthy front teeth with the gold crowns so everyone could see that he obeyed the demands of the latest style. Uncle Stephen was a revered person; he could allow himself that. He was a director of the beef industry in our capital city; therefore, he certainly needed gold teeth since he had to smile at people if he wanted them to buy his meat. During my college years, every time I looked at my uncle, I too wished that I possessed gold teeth and have his laugh. I would not even mind replacing my healthy teeth with the gold ones, but the only problem was I could not afford a gold smile. It cost about 120 rubles a tooth, more than what I made a month.

Once a month a dentist used to visit, not our but the next village, which was seven kilometers away. He could not visit our village because we neither had a building nor the appropriate equipment for him. We shared our six-room hospital with them, in addition to two other villages; they had to share their dental office with us. We were proud of our hospital, but still our village was considered the worst in the country. And if that were not enough—it was on the border with Poland. From our biggest hill, we could actually see Polish people working on their fields. Our village feared them because they often crossed our border to do us harm—or so it was told by our frontier guard. We called them stupid Polaks or spies. We also feared that some day they would cross our border and kill us all because our village used to belong Poland, but right before World War II it became a part of us. We knew they wanted their land back. Often a bunch of soldiers ran through our village with dogs, asking questions as to whether we had spotted some Polaks. I never saw any spy, and even back then I could not understand why they would want our village.

The biggest building in our village was a frontier post, much bigger than our hospital; it had two floors and about twelve rooms. It was almost as big as the White House at the end of the nineteenth century, before the West Wing was built. Perhaps because of the frontier post, our village was pretty closed to outsiders. And maybe for that reason we were so excited about our bread truck. The guards had another truck. Unlike the bread truck it was strong and drove right across the ruts in our road and never even once got stuck there. Our fathers were never called to the street to help this truck get to its final destination. But who needed our fathers anyway? The truck was always loaded with soldiers. Some soldiers were friendly to us and used to give us rides to school, which too was located in the next village. Our village had four grades only. From fifth to eight grade we went to the one that was located seven kilometers away from ours. In order to graduate from high school, we needed to go to yet another village, ten kilometers away.

On the day when the dentist came to town, everyone who had problems with their teeth—you had a tooth problem if you could not eat or drink anything because of the tooth pain—would gather, old and young, in our only community house and together went to see the dentist have their teeth pulled. It was our Canterbury trip, and some rode on top of braided horses, some walked. Others, the youngest and oldest, sat in the wagons of harnessed horses. Similar wagons can still be seen on the streets of Atlantic City, carrying the retired seniors from one casino to another. The line was always so long that people had to stay there for more than five hours. Almost everyone brought lard and bread with them for lunch—lard and bread were the most popular snack in our village, as pizza is for Italians—because once you missed your place in line, you were gone. If someone tried to sneak in front, well, others would pull out those people's teeth without even the dentist's help. When my old aunt—the same one who always stood in the bread line for a second time—tried to let her sister stay next to her in line, since she was closer to the door, both got their scarves pulled from their heads along with a handful of hair by several stronger women.

I stood in such a line once, too, when I was about twelve because I had a cavity in one of my molars, but I never made it on that day. I had to wait another month. But because I had so much pain, my father took me to our next-door neighbor, who pulled teeth when a professional dentist was not around. I can still clearly see the rusted pliers in his hands. He examined the pliers for a while, scratched some rust from it with his index and thumb nails, and wiped it on his slacks. Then he took a bottle of vodka from the kitchen cabinet, poured a bit of it in a glass cup, and stuck the pliers in the alcohol, holding them there for a few seconds. I had no idea why he did that, but he said it was meant to kill all the bugs. I did not see any bug there, but he said that some were very small. Only then did he tell me to open my mouth. I felt the cold pliers touching my gums. I no longer remember the pain, but I can still see my father holding my head against his chest while he was moving his hand round and round, then up and down before my eyes. I also remember a lot of blood, which made it difficult for him to extract my tooth completely. The tooth broke, and he could no longer pull out all the pieces. He kept wiping my mouth with a towel, but he could not see what he was doing because the blood would not stop. In the end he told my father that it was OK because even if it was broken, I would not have a toothache anymore. He also told me that the pain would stop. It did not, though, and five days later my father had to take me to the county hospital, two hundred kilometers away from the village, because my face had swollen up so much that I could hardly open my right eye.

Perhaps because of that, I became so tough that even now I do not have anesthesia when my dentist does my fillings. Had I continued to live in my village, by today I would not have any tooth of my own. People rarely got their fillings in our village even though they were available. It was much easier to just extract their teeth. It was faster and the pain only lasted for a few seconds. Anesthesia was never available for fillings though; there was this notion among our dentists that it would not be able to deaden the nerve. For that reason when I had a root canal while in college, I had nothing, not even a glass of vodka.

Another reason why fillings were not popular in our village was that the dentist could serve only a certain number of people. Going to that office, we promised each other to be quick so everyone in need would get help on the same day. So teeth pulling worked better for us. Often there was no pain at all because we could have chosen to be anaesthetized. Though, even with anesthesia, I never had any painless memory in my tooth-extracting experience, which happened five times. Particularly the incident with my neighbor pulling out my tooth made me really care about my mouth. It made me look at other people's teeth as well. When I became older, I started to notice how bad my father's teeth truly were, but he did not even care at all about them.

His lack of faith in the toothbrush drove me insane. It would not have been such a big deal had he kept his conviction to himself, but he did not. Every time he saw me brushing my teeth, I felt as if I had robbed a bank. Therefore, I usually brushed them when he was not around. Once, though, when I was about sixteen, my father spotted me brushing my teeth in the kitchen in a small bucket. There was no other place. I could brush them in the kitchen or outside since our house did not have a bathroom inside. Though we did have a twenty-gallon tub where I used to take baths. But the tub always stood under the kitchen table, and we were not allowed to take it out until our Saturday night bath day. Neither did we have a sink in our kitchen. Only during my final year of college did my family finally buy a sink, and it stood on the porch. It was one of those sinks that had to be filled with a bucket of water while another bucket had to be placed underneath the sink so that dirty water could flow out. After the bucket was full, my mother had to pour the water outside, usually by our outhouse. I was happy for my parents that they had moved up in the world, and that they now washed their faces in the morning in the sink instead of with a cup of water drawn from the kitchen bucket.

It would be another five or so years before my family bought a sink, so in the meantime I had to brush my teeth in the kitchen bucket. When my father spotted me brushing my teeth, it was evening, one of winter's minus 25-degree-Celsius days. It was so cold that your mucus would freeze in an instant both outside and inside your nose. My father and his neighbor friend Mr. Myzak, my boyfriend's father, happily chatted in the kitchen playing dominoes. Every time my father blocked him from putting a domino into the game, he knitted his brow and band his fists together. Being two feet taller and almost twice heavier than my father, he did not like to be clobbered by some lilliputian. But my father was so confident in himself that he kept showing Mr. Myzak all of his molar teeth, and I could even see that he had had red kidney beans for dinner.

On a warmer day I would have taken a cup of water and a toothbrush with paste on it and jumped outside, just to avoid a confrontation with my father, but I could not do it on this cold evening. Instead, I decided to brush my teeth inside; I needed to because I was supposed to go on a date a half an hour later. I waited for as long as I could for my father to leave the kitchen. However, as an old clock ticked on the kitchen wall, I felt certain that my father would be there for the whole evening. I could not miss even a second of its tick because it was loud; it was a huge twenty-inch clock from feudal times. It seemed to me that the clock was running fast on purpose, and my boyfriend Semen was probably waiting for me outside already. So I had no other choice but to brush my teeth in front of my father.

I figured that my father would not even notice me. He seemed so preoccupied with winning his game of dominoes that he did not even turn his head when I walked in the kitchen. So I quickly unscrewed the cap on the toothpaste tube, squeezed the paste evenly on the entire brush, and gently, quietly so as not to let the noise from brushing call his attention, started to scrub my teeth. I glanced at him one more time before starting to brush hard, but it appeared to me that he had lost himself in the domino game. I felt safe, so safe that I increased the speed and drove the brush a little harder on my teeth. Had I continued to move the brush gently, none of what was to come might have happened. I had made a big mistake. The noise of the toothbrush had the same effect on my father as the noise of the drilling machine in a dentist office on the small children. It suddenly provoked my father to the point where he stopped playing dominoes and dropped one of his six-six's on the floor. Instead of picking it up, he switched all his attention from the game to my mouth. Perhaps, had the neighbor not been sitting in the kitchen, he would not have said anything. However, brushing teeth in front of just not any but the most respectable of our neighbors, my father's best and only true friend, was not acceptable for him.

Being totally absorbed, I did not immediately discern that the game had ceased. While with great enjoyment and pride I was brightening my teeth, moving the brush back and forth, then round and round, then spitting the remaining paste into the bucket, I suddenly realized that there was no other noise in the kitchen besides the noise of my toothbrush. On the back of my head I felt that my father was looking at me. I blushed and turned my head, still holding the toothbrush in my mouth, towards the kitchen table. I was right; he was staring at me. After holding his gaze on additional seconds, he finally lost his temper and said: "You should be ashamed of yourself! It's embarrassing to brush your teeth, especially in front of other people!" It was embarrassing, indeed, because I was on the spot in front of the neighbor whose son I really liked. It was his son with whom I would have a date in only a few minutes, and for whom I was preparing my teeth with such a boldness and desperation, almost before my father's eyes. But still, no matter how humiliated I was, I decided to defend myself and stormed right back at him: "It's embarrassing not to brush your teeth," I said and left the room. And ever since that time I had not been able to forgive him, not just for embarrassing me, but for not taking care of his teeth.

***

My father had never in his lifetime even held a toothbrush in his hand, and his teeth had everything stuck in them: chunks of old food that were just about to grow in and become an inseparable part of his teeth; tiny grains of brown tobacco that were noticeable when he smiled; black cavity spots that could be detected all over his mouth; and sometimes even broken pieces of matches that he used to retrieve old food stuck in his large cavities. From time to time he liked to break a match in half and stick the sharpest half of it in his forward incisors.

43

Then he would take another match and without breaking it, cautiously and gently, as if not to invoke pain, direct it to his molars. He enjoyed depositing matches inside his teeth as much as I enjoyed sticking toothbrushes in my mouth, though both of us had different reasons for doing so. I wanted to have a clean smile. My father wanted to stop the pain from cavities. He thought that if he could get the food remains out of his teeth, the pain would go away. Often he even ate a lot of cheese and garlic because his best friend had told him that cheese would prevent cavities and keep the teeth healthy while garlic would take the pain away.

I could not take this nonsense any more and had given up on him. Often I was in disgust and deemed his teeth to be a storage room, a rainbow storage room containing hues from all the primary colors.

Perhaps for that reason I never tried to become closer to my father during my adolescence; I was embarrassed by him, especially when I left our small village and farm for the big city and college. Living in the city for me was like living in a wonderland. My dormitory had running water from seven to nine in the morning and from six to eleven at night. I had a kitchen with gas stove, which I shared with twelve other people, but it was still very impressive for me because it would take my parents approximately an hour and half a canister of petroleum to ignite the wet wood. While in my dormitory, I could have a fire in just a second, with a small turn of a knob. We also had one bathroom on each floor. We even had a shower in the building. It was good too because I no longer needed to wash myself in a twenty-gallon tub. I could now take a shower twice a week; I did not even mind the wait in line, which was not that long, usually an hour or two. I knew immediately that I was born for the city life.

Often my father visited me in the dormitory to bring me some food to make sure I was not hungry. I wished my mother would come instead, but she could not because she was always busy taking care of the farm animals and cooking. Of course my father did the most work around the farm, but he could not cook. No man in my village ever prepared a meal. Even Peter's dinners were cooked by his neighbors once in a while. When some men's wives died, their daughters or daughter-in-laws had to cook for them because the oldest sons or daughters usually stayed with their parents after they got married. If there were no sons or daughters, the relatives or friends would cook for the widowers.

So my mother did not have time to visit me. It was not as if she could make enough *pirogies* or soup for three days and stuff them in the refrigerator. Not many people even knew what that word meant; therefore, fresh meals had to be cooked every single day. Leftovers were fed to the animals.

No longer considering myself a farm girl, I did not want my father to visit me. I was uncomfortable taking two old reused plastic bags—similar to the ones we get in a supermarket or department store in the United States—with food from his hands, especially in front of my roommates. They never said anything inappropriate to him, but instead always talked and smiled to him more than I ever did and asked him all kinds of questions as to how people lived on the farm, where they took their showers, what they did with so many animals, and why they kept their dogs on a leash. My father, eager to explain everything to them, replied with a smile—perhaps wondering how someone could possibly not know the answer to those questions—that we needed to keep so many animals because some had to be sold, others eaten, still others kept for reproduction. He then wanted to go to the next question until I reminded him that I needed to rush to the library to do my research projects. I just knew he was like an alien to them or as if they had just discovered a young Victor in the wild. Quickly, my hands trembling, I took the food from the bags, put it on the table without looking at it, and returned his bags to him immediately because I knew he would not forget to ask me: "Can you give me back those bags so I can use them the next time? Your mother will ask me for them. You know." I did know that. I was the one who supplied those bags for them from the black market. Bags were an item not only in my village but in the whole country. No store ever, during my time, packed people's food or clothes in bags. The best our government could come up with was paper. Newspapers served our villages; brownish paper towels—like the one we wipe our hands with in *Wal Mart* bathrooms—were prevalent in the cities.

We needed to bring our own bags to the store; thousands of them, though, were available on the black market for a ruble each. Even *Macy's*, *J.C.Penney*, and *K-Mart* bags could be found there. We just did not know what they represented. But it was fashionable to carry imported bags. I often bought six for my parents, but they tried to use the same two all the time. Both my mother and father got upset when their bags ripped. My mother tried all kinds of tricks to prolong their usefulness. When the handle slit in two, she'd knot it. If that did not work, she would still assign my father the same bag, but he needed to put his hand underneath it to support it. The bags in which my father brought food for me often had a number of tiny holes on their sides, and no one could distinguish whether those were foreign or domestic.

I always knew what was inside of those bags: a whole broiled or cooked chicken or duck, a pound of sour cream, a wheel of farmer's cheese, and a dozen eggs, each coarsely wrapped in newspaper or my old elementary school books in one bag; ten potatoes, five apples, and six pears or plums in the other. When my father was ready to leave, he would always take ten rubles from his old wallet and hand them to me, and from his pocket he would extract my old favorite, a bit smashed, a Danish, which I no longer liked, and awkwardly with a wobble of his hand back and forth and then after some pause pass it to me saying: "Here is your *corszick*."

I wish I could take that *corszick* and all that other food from my father's hand now, but back then his gifts made me uncomfortable because I did not know what my friends would think of me. I thought that seeing him and the country food, my friends would discover all over my secret of being a farmer's daughter—which I feared the most—as if they could not figure it out from my clothes. I hated everything about my life on the farm, and I still had the same wish as in my childhood—to have a better father. My friends' fathers were lawyers, doctors, teachers, and engineers who had marvelous clothes and smelled of deodorants and perfumes every time they visited their daughters. My father did not even wear a suit. His fingernails were dirty from the farm, his shoes bore dried clay from the village's unasphalted muddy roads, his jacket was wrinkled, his dark brown fedora was old and out of fashion, his light brown leather backpack that his brother from America had sent him fifty years ago was so damaged that it was even impossible to tell that the backpack was made out of natural animal skin. I smelled the farm every time my father walked inside my room.

My father knew that I was ashamed of him because he never stayed longer than half an hour inside my room, even when there was nobody but just the two of us. And when I would say to him, "Don't go yet. Your bus is not leaving for another four hours," tacitly hoping he would leave, he would give me the same answer all the time: "I have to go because I must buy some tomatoes and cucumbers for your mother. I must also visit Uncle Stephen."

Then I would kiss him, lightly touching his cheek, and without further objections let him go. And he would depart and spend the remaining four hours outside looking at the tall buildings and observing the high-speed traffic of automobiles, trolleys, and tramways, never even visiting Uncle Stephen but, instead, walking back and forth along the same street in order not to get lost and be late for his bus back to the village, his farm, and the only home he had ever known. Every time I saw Uncle Stephen and told him that my father had visited me, he was surprised that my father had not come to see him.

Often I felt sorry for my father, and many times I have regretted that I did not let him stay longer in my room, which I shared with two other girls. It is hard to believe that three people would live together in a single fifteen-by-twenty-foot room for five years, but we did. We had three separate beds, two on the opposite side from each other, the last right behind the one that stood on the left side of the window. When last year I visited Alcatraz prison, the prisoners' rooms reminded me of my dormitory, except we that did not have iron bars on our doors. We did not have a toilet in our room either. We possessed, though, two tables, five chairs, and one small closet where each of us had a separate chest for our clothes. I still liked my dorm better than my farmhouse because it had a sink and a toilet inside the building.

Of course there was not much room for my father to stay in my room, but every time I let him wander on the streets before his bus finally arrived, I promised myself that next time I would be nicer to him. But that next time never came somehow, and I kept putting it off for just a little longer. I knew that my father would like me to make him a cup of tea. It would make him so happy that he would tell my mother all about how I made it for him, had given him a piece of bread with butter, and had even fried him eggs mixed with mashed potatoes. And my mother would be happy too to hear that her Anita had learned how to be on her own, that she was such a good girl, and that she even had learned how to cook.

I rarely asked my father to have tea; I did so only when my friends were not around. I especially did not want my boyfriend Michael to see my father. What would he think about me if he saw my father's teeth? Even if my father could hide his teeth, he could not have hidden his old-fashioned polyester clothes from the late sixties and early seventies, his ungentle, uncultivated village manners, his burned-by-the sun dark-skinned unshaven face, his chopped hands, peeling from dryness, and his dialect, which my new city beau would not even understand.

Michael perhaps had never even seen a real farmer. He was the fifth generation of a city-born family—government employees. His grandfathers and great-grandfathers had been tax collectors; his father, an accountant for the same collection agency, except he had to pledge his allegiance to three different flags every time a new regime took over his city. For some reason Michael did not follow in his clan's footsteps. He was a capitalist at heart and wanted to own everything he could lay his hands on. I did not exactly know what his job was. I doubt whether he had ever graduated from college; he would not have had the patience to study boring dead men's books filled with rosy propaganda about the prosperity of socialism. He told me once that college was for ignorant people and those who could not make it in the world. He was a businessman, but I never saw him working. Not even once did I see him rushing to his workplace on Monday morning the way the rest of the city people did. But I always heard him talking about his business, at a time when people could not even own their houses. He must have had other people performing his dirty duties since his hands were as clean and soft as fresh snow. His fingernails were always cut short and buffed. Michael never used any cologne; he used deodorant instead, unlike many other men I knew. He said that real men did not use perfumes. I liked that about him; I also liked that I never smelled any bad odor from his body. He had Arnold's body and look, and for that reason it would be an honor for every woman in the city to walk next to him on the street. They could not even dream about holding his hand or trying to win themselves a date with him. I had no idea why he had picked me.

My boyfriend knew that I was a village girl. He just always thought I was the principal's daughter. I thought it appropriate to make up all kinds of stories about my father since neither of them had any chance of being introduced to each other in the future. I recognized that my boyfriend would never marry me, not in a hundred years, though I wanted to be his wife more than anything in the world. I actually thought that about every boyfriend I ever had. Yet, every time I met someone better looking, I kept changing my mind. But this, I contemplated, for certain, was different. He was my forbidden apple. Eve was better off than I was, though; at least she could bite it. I could not. I had nothing to offer him. Successful women were crazy about him; their fathers supplied him with cars, apartments, and money. The most my father could offer in exchange for me would be some land, horses, cows, and pig's meat, but who needed those in the city, except for the pork roast? Accepting the reality that I would not be his wife, I still had my fantasies and thought he was the one. Somewhere on the back of my heart I left a note for myself: "If not him, then nobody."

He liked me, of course, but only as someone with whom he could feel like a real man. He liked my inexperience, innocence, and maybe appearance, but he was open about having other relationships. I did not mind as long as he kept visiting me at least twice a week. I also liked it because he told me I could call him my boyfriend; while others were denied that opportunity.

Once my boyfriend saw me with my father walking on the street while he was riding a bus. My boyfriend was so excited to see me that he started to knock on the bus window to get me to notice and wait for him at the bus stop. Instead of waiting for him, I ran away, abandoning my father on the middle of the street. It was the only time I really wanted to accompany him to the bus station, but again it never happened. Instead, I had to fabricate yet another excuse to get rid of him. I told him that I had totally forgotten I had a meeting with my professor in about twenty minutes, and he would have to walk to the bus station himself this time. But I promised to walk him another time for certain. My father did not question me; his only concern was that I was going to be late for that meeting. He urged me to rush there as fast as I could and worry about nothing else besides my appointment.

Unlike my father, my boyfriend questioned me, but I pretended that

I had never seen him on the bus. When he came to visit me that night and asked me why I had not waited for him, and who that old man was walking behind me, I answered: "I didn't see you on any bus," and I changed the subject immediately, never answering his second question. I got off easily because he did not insist on finding out about the old man after I kissed him on his lips. I could kiss him as much as I wanted on that day since my roommates were out. It was mandatory for others to get out when someone's boyfriend showed up. I myself often spent several hours in the kitchen to let my girlfriends be alone with their boyfriends. And since all the visitors were allowed to stay in the building until nine p.m., nobody minded giving another some privacy.

But at night when I lay in bed, I thought about my farmhouse and about my father. I knew now that he was a good person. In a way he was like a child, so uncorrupted. When he walked on the city's streets, he used to say hi to every person who looked at him. He did not just utter a regular hi but took off his hat, bowed a little, and said out loud, "Praise Jesus Christ"—that is how people in my village greeted each other. When they would not answer him "Praise forever," he wondered why were they so rude as not to give glory to God. I told him once, "Dad, people in the city do not greet each other the way villagers do. They do not say hi to strangers."

Then he would say to me, "But he must have known me from somewhere because he looked at me."

I would bite my lips, groaning through my teeth, "Dad, how can someone possibly know you in the city? Do you know how many people live here?"

He would just say, "But maybe he did know me. Remember I sold five chickens at the market here last month. Maybe he bought it from me." After a few months I finally persuaded him not to say hi to anyone in the city, to which he agreed.

This episode actually made me like him a bit more because I was slowly beginning to realize that my father was just a simple person and relatively uneducated farmer, and that some day I would have to accept him for who he was. It was still too far for me to go because I was not willing to let my friends meet him on regular bases. What if, seeing him again, they changed their minds about me? It had taken me almost two years to finally be accepted; I could not let my luck slip away now when my friends had begun to accept me to the point that they would even invite me to the most fancy nightclubs in the city. I could not allow my father to ruin my life. It often seemed to me that he visited me on purpose to remind me about home and where I came from, which I hated because I felt that I was beyond my father's farm. I was only someone who had been born there, nothing more. The whole notion of "farm" gave me creepy feelings. I had another, much better, intellectual city life.

I thought that if he really loved me, he could at least put on clean shoes, take off his dopey hat, and iron his clothes or buy himself a suit so he could look decent when he visited me. I knew I judged him too harshly. I also knew that no matter what I did, he would still come back to me with his two bags of country food. And I knew as well that I could never make him understand that I was the victim and not him because I had to stay and live with my friends. He would have never understood how hard I had worked to secure my present spot among the city people. I knew that my father's reputation would not be ruined if I let him go; it was I who would suffer in the end if my friends looked closely at my father's teeth. I was the one who would have to deal with my friends for a long time.

Other thoughts occupied my mind from time to time too. Why did city people have such a terrible attitude towards villagers, and why could my father not be just like my roommates' fathers? I wished I could hold my father's hand, walking proudly with him on the street and carrying my head up. I wished I could hug him at least once and embrace his shoulders tight without letting him go for a long time. But I could not. It was his fault that he never brushed his teeth, never cared about his appearance, had never taught me how to ride a horse, had never taken me to school on my first day the way other fathers did, had never talked with me about serious matters when I became sixteen as to what I wanted to do with my life and what profession I might choose for myself so my life would be better than his, never even put a hand on my shoulder and told me that he loved me.

My mind was full of all kinds of questions about my father. Some of them changed over time and acquired new meaning; others were forgotten. At nights I felt guilty and could not sleep, but during the day—especially when I observed other fathers—I just could not forgive

51

him for being a farmer. One question always occupied my mind, "Why can he not be like other fathers?"

***

By the end of my college years my mind was set. I was convinced that I was not special to my father nor was he for me, and there was nothing more between us than just regular family ties. I did not even wish to visit the farm, and I would show up there once a month, if that. My father too appeared less and less frequently in my dormitory because he knew that I did not need his food any longer. However, I was still receiving the weekly ten rubles by priority mail from him.

Soon, even that would change because I graduated from collage and got my first teaching job. And even though I lived in the city and had obtained a job that I liked, I was still dissatisfied with my life because I could never compete with my city friends who possessed their own houses and a lot of money. I wished that my father would send me ten rubles again because I could hardly afford to pay my rent from my miserable monthly wages. It would be embarrassing to ask him for money now; so I never did. Instead, I tried to find different ways to compete with my friends, and I truly believed that some day I would catch up with them. The perfect way finally opened to me.

My country was collapsing before everyone's eyes. The borders were open. The Berlin Wall was torn down. Reagan visited Moscow and welcomed everyone to come to America to see how people lived under capitalism. People right and left were leaving my country. All of a sudden I too remembered that I had an uncle in the United States. After I wrote him a letter, he immediately responded, inviting me to come visit him. America, the land of opportunity!

A year later, after all my documents were finally complete, I was leaving my home, farm, father, and country forever. The day before the trip I lightly, as usual, kissed my father on the cheek when I was ready to say goodbye.

My mother had cried the whole morning. She told me that she had a feeling that I would never come back home and again reminded me about the dying lady's prophecy.

"That's what she meant. You would go to America and become famous there," she said and started to look at my fingers. Then she took them in her hands and said, "She was right, look at those fingers! They

52

are so long, artistic, easily bent. She was right. Look at my fingers, I can do nothing with them. And look at yours. You can still reach your wrist with you thumb. I always knew that lady was right," she said, kissing each of my fingers, which reminded me about the times she did her whispering over me to get rid of my intestinal worms.

I looked at her fingers. They were hunched, with their edges beveled down, wrinkled, even though she was only fifty-five. Then I looked into her eyes. They were watery, brown. Her small, delicate yellowish nose, now, was red. Her pitted chin was trembling. I saw no dimples on her bony cheeks. At the place where the kerchief did not cover her dark brown hair, above her forehead, I could see several gray ones. Her lean agreeable figure now looked smaller, just about like my father's, even though she was a few inches taller than he. I always considered my father an old man, though he was in fact five years older than she. Perhaps it was because of his gray hair. Now I knew she was getting old, and I did not want to remember her this way. I wanted to see her as this bouncy brisk woman I knew in my childhood, running towards me to the outhouse, waving her hands, wiping them in her apron, and at the same time fixing her silk kerchief that was just about to slide down from her head to her neck. But no matter how much I tried to eradicate the memory of my mother sitting in the kitchen chair on the day I was leaving, I can still see her that way, with those gray hairs on her brown head.

Looking up at the ceiling, I laughed, assuring her that I would never become famous nor stay permanently in a country whose language I did not even understand. No matter what I did, I could not stop her from crying. She even had trouble frying a chicken for me so I would have something to eat on the train to Moscow. The chicken burned, and my mother asked my father to kill another one. I personally had to take off the burned skin from the chicken to persuade my mother that the chicken was perfectly fine to eat.

My father did not cry. He stayed outside most of the time. As it got closer to twelve he kept coming in and out every five minutes or so. He must have said three times that he had to go out to feed his horse. Another five minutes passed. My father was inside again. I got up and went to my room to check my luggage one final time. Everything was packed. I sat on my bed looking in my five-inch mirror and putting on lipstick. I noticed my father slowly opening my door. He stood there for a while buttressing my door and mashing his hat in his hands while he looked at it. Then he finally looked at me.

"Can I go with you to the city? At least to the train station? So...I can help you with your luggage?"

"No, it's five hours of driving, Father. If you miss your bus, how are you going to get back home?"

"I can sleep at the train station."

"No, I'll say goodbye now," I answered and left the room. Half an hour later I was gone.

A lot of my friends came to the local train station to say goodbye. There were Mary, Irene, Lidia, Valerie, Anna, Swetlana, and Michael. My brother Willy was there too, who did not become a farmer despite the fact that my father had put so much effort into making him one. When he turned sixteen, my father wanted to give him one of his horses on his birthday. My brother told him, "Dad, I don't like horses. I want to be a scientist. I want to go to college." My father sold the horse, two cows, and a bull and sent my brother to college. Much later he became well known and respected in my country as a biologist even though his fingers were not as artistic as mine, but as straight as a ruler. And to everybody but me he is Dr. William Matkowsky. Not surprisingly he had been after my village's frogs and grasshoppers ever since he could feel the ground under his feet. I guess the dying lady got it all wrong. She should have died about five years later. Now, since my brother too lived in the city, he came to say goodbye. Everybody was there, except my father.

There was much crying and laughing at the train station that day. There were many promises on my and my friend's sides to write letters to each other, to never forget, and to come back soon, within two years, as soon as I made enough money to buy an apartment. But just as I was ready to step onto the train, I recognized the most familiar figure in my life—a small man with a light brown backpack and a dark brown fedora. Desperately, slipping to the ground, bumping his shoes on the course rocks, and hitting other people with his elbows and backpack, the man was running from one car to another looking for someone.

"Father!" I screamed with all the force I could gather from my lungs.

All of my friends turned their heads towards my father, who stopped running, feeling guilty that his presence among my friends would embarrass me. I glanced at my friends. I noticed that Swetlana's and Michael's mouths were open. I also noticed wrinkles on their foreheads, and their faces appeared strange and fake. They meant nothing to me anymore.

I ran towards my father, leaving all of them behind.

"What are you doing here?" I asked him with my eyes full of tears.

"You forgot this," and he handed me a piece of badly wrinkled paper.

I opened the paper and saw a note, which had been sent to me by my American uncle on how to make a phone call in case we missed each other at Kennedy Airport.

"But that's an extra copy. I have another one with me," I answered softly.

"I know. I just thought…I just…I just wanted to see you one more time."

I did not know what to say to him; all I wanted was for him to be next to me. It was the first time in my life that I had not been embarrassed of my father. For the first time I was not embarrassed to see him among my friends and my boyfriend. I wanted to talk to him, but no words would come out of my mouth. Instead, I hugged him tightly for the first time in my life, and for the first time I truly did not want him to leave. Now he was the one who told me that it was time to go. I wiped my tears into his shoulder and silently walked into the train, for the first time being confident that I was a special daughter, a father's daughter.

Printed in the United States
16220LVS00001B/40-42

9 781413 708387